D0984179

DATE DUE

3 117

INFERNAL
PARADE

INFERNAL
PARADE

CLIVE BARKER

SUBTERRANEAN PRESS 2017

First Edition

ISBN
978-1-59606-807-0

Subterranean Press
PO Box 190106
Burton, MI 48519

subterraneanpress.com

Table of Contents

Tom
Requiem

THOUGH THERE HAD been men in recent history who had committed crimes far worse than those of Tom Requiem, none drew the crowds the size of those who came to the Requiem Trial. The reason? Tom was a star. He knew how to smile, he knew how to look penitent, he knew when to play the fool, and when to simply do nothing, and leave his admirers to project upon his beautiful face all that they wanted to see there.

Some saw Christ. With his long dark curly hair, and the rough beard he'd grown in prison, Requiem did indeed look like the Man of Sorrows in certain lights.

What he *didn't* look like was a man who killed a woman in a sordid back-street squabble over the dividing of the profit from an afternoon of pick-pocketing. But as the prosecution reminded the jury over and over, Requiem's many faces were not to be trusted. He was a Guizer, said the lawyer, a man who took pleasure in putting on faces to suit the occasion, not one of them more trustworthy than any other.

"I have heard men grow pale when they hear of Tom Requiem's reputation as a great fighter, and tender hearted women blush when they hear stories of his prowess as a lover, but when we come to inquire as to where these stories originate, what do we find? Why, that they have come from the lips of the great lover himself. He is a liar, born and bred, a man who likes nothing better than to weave fabrications and fantastications, and make the world his fool by having us believe them! This, ladies and gentlemen of the jury, I will prove today, as I uncover his crimes and deceits. By the time I am done telling you the truth about Thomas Absalom Requiem you will find very little to admire about him, I'll wager, and much to hold in the profoundest contempt."

Prosecutors are not always good at doing as they promise they'll do, but this one was an exception. By the time the lengthy trial was over, Tom Requiem's many reputations were in tatters. His female conquests had come into the witness box and given lists of his inadequacies, while those he had reputedly fought against in human combat told of his street-dog tricks.

"There you have it then," said the prosecutor. "Tom Requiem is a cheat, a philanderer and a murderer. He may have an innocent look on his face right now but I beg you—be not deceived!—he is fully deserving of the hangman's noose."

The jury agreed, and the judge declared the next day that Tom Requiem would be hanged by the neck until dead. And God have mercy on his soul.

That night, well after midnight, Tom had a visitor. He introduced himself as Joshua Kemp; he was to be Tom's hangman.

"I will be merciful," Kemp said, "for I see no purpose in prolonging a man's agony." He drew closer to Tom as he spoke, and glanced back over his shoulder to be certain that nobody was listening at the door. "But," he said, lowering his voice in a whisper, "should you find by some wild chance that I did not complete tomorrow's business—"

"What are you saying?"

"Keep your voice down and listen. There are those parties who would like to see you preserved from so short a life."

"Well, well," said Tom. "Not that I'm not grateful an' all, but why would anybody work to save my sorry neck from the noose?"

Kemp tugged at the collar of his shirt, as though this subject was growing a little too uncomfortable for *him*. "Better I don't talk about that," he said. "I just came here to tell you to take courage and for God's sake, *play dead*. You may be buried, but you'll be dug up again. That's a promise."

"Buried…alive?" Tom Requiem murmured.

"That's the word to keep remembering," the hangman said. "*Alive. Alive.*"

"Oh, I'll remember," Tom replied.

SO THE NEXT day, with his head shorn of its shiny locks, and his chest shaved clean, Tom Requiem was taken to the gallows, where a huge crowd waited to see judgment done. Despite his conversation with Kemp of the previous night, he did not feel much reassured. He watched the hangman's face—right up until the moment when the burlap sack was put over his head—searching for some sign, however small, of reassurance. A wink, a tiny smile.

But there was nothing but sweat on Kemp's face. Then the bag came down like a black curtain, and Tom heard himself breathing hard in darkness. The murmur of the crowd receded to near silence. The priest came to the end of his prayer. There was clatter, and a terrible emptiness beneath his feet. Then he fell, down and down, and the darkness became a blaze of white, so bright that it burned all his thoughts away.

What happened then was all fragments, coming and going. He saw faces, looking down at him, contemptuous faces, laughing faces. He saw a doctor come and give him a cursory glance (a doctor, it should be said, with a most peculiar look in his eye, as though there were many fires burning in his head), and then apparently dismissing him as a dead thing; as worthless. All that was easy enough to take. What followed was not. What followed was the stuff of nightmares, and in that tiny place in his head where Tom Requiem was still alive he was a tiny ball of fear. To see the coffin sides rising around him as he was put in that plain wooden box! To see the lid slid into place, eclipsing the last of the light, until there was nothing, nothing, nothing to see but darkness! To hear the wood creak around him as the coffin was carried to the grave, and the sound of the digging, and the raw rasp of the ropes as they were hauled beneath the box to drop it down into the grave! And finally—oh worst of all, the very worst!—the sound of the earth rattling down onto the lid of the coffin, becoming more and more muffled as the grave filled up, until there was no sound at all. Nothing!

It had all been a terrible trick, he began to think. This was his enemies' way of revenging themselves on him.

Death hadn't been enough. They'd wanted to try him by hope, leaving him alive in the grave, knowing that eventually he would lose his sanity.

He could feel it slipping away, moment by moment, heartbeat by heartbeat. There he had nothing to pray to in his darkness. No God that he believed in. No loving Virgin Mother who would have forgiven him his trespasses. He was beyond all help.

Or was he?

What was that sound in the earth?

Somebody digging, was it?

Did he dare believe that after all somebody *was* going to come and save him from this place of torments? Or was it just his crazed mind playing tricks on him? Yes, that it was! It was just one last proof of his insanity, because, listen, listen, the sound wasn't even coming from above, it was coming from below!

Ridiculous. How could anybody be digging towards him from *below*?

And yet…and yet…

The more he listened, the more he seemed to hear the sound of shovels cutting through dirt, and voices even, the voices of the diggers, getting louder as they approached.

Finally, he heard a spade strike against the board beneath him. The coffin reverberated. He wanted to weep with relief. He was going to be saved! The question remained as to what manner of creature would dig a man out of his grave from below, but frankly he didn't much care: a savior was a savior, whatever shape it came in, and from whatever direction.

Now he felt hands on the coffin from all sides; and people talking all around. He couldn't make sense of what they were saying, but some of them were perhaps giving orders, for a few seconds later several powerful instruments (perhaps crowbars) were tearing at the underside of his coffin. Light broke through, yellow light, and finally the bottom of the coffin was removed completely, and he dropped into the arms of those who had worked to save him.

There were three of them, small, quick-eyed creatures, with painted faces. They introduced themselves. Clovio, Heeler and Bleb.

But it wasn't the diggers who claimed most of Tom Requiem's attention, it was their master. He knew the man, though not his name. This was the fellow whom Tom had presumed to be a doctor, who had briefly examined him before he was committed to the grave. No wonder he had spotted no sign of life in the hanged man. He'd been in the plot all along.

His eyes burned brighter now, and when they fixed their gaze on "the dead man" Tom felt the rigidities of death fall away, and life flooded back into his body, from scalp to sole.

"Welcome," said the Doctor. "No doubt you are surprised to see me down here."

"Yeah. I guess I am," Tom said. His voice was low from the constriction his windpipe had lately taken, but the Doctor had a quick cure for that.

"Drink this!" he said, handing a silver flask to Requiem.

Never one for half measures, Tom knocked back two full throatfuls of the liquor, which coursed through his cold body most pleasantly.

"We haven't brought you down here into the Underland out of simple compassion, Tom," the Doctor went on.

"No?"

"No, we have work for you to do. We will dress you in a costume befitting a shaman, and you will go out into the world to lead an Infernal Parade. The world has grown complacent, Tom; and fat with its own certainties. It's time to send some fears into the hearts of men."

Tom thought of the crowd that had assembled in such howling numbers to see him hanged by the neck until dead.

"It will be my pleasure," he said. "Where do I begin?"

"With the woman whose life you took," said the Doctor. With Mary Slaughter…"

Mary
Slaughter

"MARY, MARY, MARY," Tom Requiem said. "Look at you. You haven't changed a bit."

"Whereas *you*, Tom, *you* look like you've been scalped and hanged and buried alive."

"Was that just a lucky guess or…?"

"Guessing games are for children," Mary said. "I believe in being in possession of all the facts. So I've made it my business to watch every little humiliation that you've had to endure since you took my life from me."

The smug smile she'd been wearing since setting eyes on him suddenly disappeared; she bared her teeth which she had sharpened, since her demise, and said:

"I watched it all. The court. The trial. All those intimate moments in the prison when you prayed for my forgiveness—"

"I never prayed!" Tom Requiem grumbled.

"Oh yes you did. You sobbed until the shit ran down your face, you were so afraid of going to Hell for your sins. And you're a lucky sonofabitch, Tom Requiem. Because plenty of people have been sent to Hell for less than what you did to me! A lot less! Other people burn in the everlasting fires for their crimes against all that is natural and loving. But you—you get to lead a parade out of the Underland and into the lives of poor dull humanity."

"Yeah…it has turned out pretty well hasn't it? I mean I can't say I didn't shit myself when I was in that damn coffin. But now…things are looking pretty good."

"Just don't think you're going to be the only one in charge of the fun and frolics. I'm joining the parade myself, to watch over you: make sure you don't step out of line."

"Oh yeah?"

"Hate the idea, do you?"

"It wouldn't be my first choice," Tom replied. "But when I think about it maybe we'll end up finding we're fond of one another again."

"That I somehow doubt." Mary Slaughter smiled.

"But you are very beautiful."

"As you remarked just a few minutes before you put your knife into my heart."

"Oh, must we talk about all this sordid stuff? It's ancient history, isn't it?"

"No, Tom, it isn't. In fact in the time since my sloughing off this mortal skin, I have educated myself in the way of blades, so that I would be ready to defend myself should you or any other cowardly, witless man attempt to do me harm."

"What harm can possibly be done to you? You're dead."

"They didn't tell you about our audience, did they?"

"No."

Mary Slaughter smiled sardonically. "We're going amongst the fallen angels, Tom. The rotted souls who gave up their place beside the Lord for a scrappy hope of revolution. That's going to be one *real* audience. And they're dangerous, Tom, they're mischief-makers. Hope destroyers. They plot night and day for some way to rise up against Heaven—?"

"I don't care."

"We will care if we get mixed up in any of their domestic politics. We could die a thousand times, believe me, at the hands of those things. It would not be pretty."

"Well then we won't go amongst them. We'll just go wherever the hell we want."

"Listen to you. As though they'd give a job to do and then trust us to do it. *The likes of us!* They know what you are, Tom: a liar and a cheat and a cut-purse."

"And what do they say about you? Adulteress?"

"Probably."

"Whore?"

"Now, now, don't get hurtful. I have tender feelings."

"You? *Tender?* You've smothered more unwanted babies and buried the mothers if they died giving birth… so don't you try to get high and mighty—not with me. It isn't going to work."

"Maybe there was some sense in making a team of us. We know each other so well—"

"And hate each other so fiercely—"

"Oh, hate's just the beginning, Tom," Mary Slaughter said, leaning towards him. "I got a thousand different feelings for you, not a single one of them pleasant."

"Well then, shall we get this show on the road?"

"First," Mary said, "don't you want to see my performance?"

"I didn't realize you had one."

"I'm not just a pretty face, Tom, unlike some I could mention. Here!" She snapped her fingers and a large wooden casket, profusely decorated with Carnival colors—bright yellows and reds, greens and golds—came sliding over the ground and stopped in front of her feet. No bird-dog could have been better trained to attend upon its mistress' summons than this casket.

"Open!" she commanded it.

The lock picked itself in less than thirty seconds. Then the casket threw open its lid and its contents rose into the air, in a bright vein-nicking array. Swords, swords, and more swords. Swords for captains, swords for butchers, swords straight as God's gaze, swords curved like a woman's back.

"As you so unkindly took from me the opportunity to have children—"

"Oh, do the dead not breed?" said Tom casually. "Pity, I'd have given it a go."

"May God rot my eyes if I ever let you inside me, Tom Requiem. As I was saying, as I can't have children, I assembled myself a family that would never grow old, nor break my heart." She called a sword to her: "Monsieur!" It flew into her hand. "Owned by Napoleon. And bloodied, more than once."

"You surprise me. What about that one? The long one!"

"Oh, my Chief? My love sword." She let Monsieur go and he took his place at her feet. The Chief, meanwhile, rose up above her head, perilously close to her. There was such size and weight to the blade that had the might that held it aloft failed for the merest moment she would have been dead in two seconds. But Mary was

28

fearless. She threw back her head and opened her lovely wet mouth.

"Come," she said.

The sword began to descend into her throat. Tom's jaw hung open staring at the sight; he could barely believe what he was seeing. For one thing the sword was so broad, and so very plainly razor sharp, that the tiniest palpitation in the woman's throat would open a wound in her esophagus, or stomach, or innards, God help her, that no surgeon would be able to fix without cutting her open from throat to—

Mary's gaze slid in the direction of her audience of one. She even managed the tiniest twitch of a smile, as she took pleasure in the mingling of awe and incomprehension on his handsome face.

But she had more to show him. Two swords had gently slid beneath her feet, and now, as if she had issued some order that Tom had failed to catch, they lifted her up, until she was standing on their points, defying the laws of life and physics. Nor was she finished there. More blades rose from the casket and performed a series of elegant motions in the air around her head and torso. Was she their victim or their mistress; a martyr to these piercing, plunging blades or their effortless commander? He could not tell. And that perhaps was the point of this spectacle, that at any moment—a slip, a misstep, and there would be blood everywhere, albeit the blood of a dead woman.

Finally, Mary touched her forefinger to the sword she had swallowed and it rose with the same glacial ease with which it had descended, and the other blades gathered themselves up like fans and returned to their resting place in the casket.

"Very impressive," Tom said. "You're going to be the hit of our show."

"I'd better be," she said, only half-joking. "It's taken me a long time to get these tricks right. I want them appreciated."

"Oh, you'll be appreciated," Tom said. "You'll be worshipped and loved. If only by me."

"Ha! You can take your love, Tom Requiem, and drown it. But your worship? That I'll take. At least until you get on the wrong side of me."

"What then?"

"What do you think, what then?" Mary Slaughter replied. "I will cut you up into so many tiny, tiny pieces that your own mother wouldn't be able to find a fragment she recognized."

And offering a little smile to sweeten the threat, she closed up her casket, saying a fond goodnight to her swords as she did so.

"When should we hit the road?" Tom said.

"First thing tomorrow morning suits me. It's a Godless world up there. The sooner they see a glimpse of the Infernal Parade, the sooner we can get them back in the pews, praying for the sanctity of their souls." She laughed at this. "If only they knew," she said, "how little that meant…"

The Golem,
Elijah

LUIS HEARD HIS father's voice barking at him, but he didn't turn back to obey his instructions. Instead he continued to walk, away from the tenements and out towards the old furnaces. They'd been cold for years now, since Luis was just a small boy. But the mountains of grey ash that the furnaces had produced during their many years of their relentless roaring life still covered the ground all around them.

It tainted everything within a hundred square miles. It blew into the tenements, and got into the food people ate there: into their eyes too, and their beds. It made their shit grey, and their skins grey and the whites of their eyes grey.

Luis hated the ash. But not as much as he hated his family. Them he hated with as much fury as his heart could muster. His father and mother, his two sisters and his older brother, they were his enemies.

"I wish they were dead, I wish they were dead..." he said to himself as he trudged towards the furnaces. With every step a cloud of grey dust erupted around his feet. It would get worse the closer to the furnaces he ventured, he knew. But he didn't care. The more distance he put between himself and his family the happier he'd be.

Night was falling. It was getting cold. So he was pleased to see a bonfire burning in the gloom ahead of him. He headed towards it. There was no sign of the fire's owner in its vicinity, but it looked to have been recently fed, because the flames were rising ten or twelve feet into the air.

Luis approached the fire and warmed himself. He was a scrawny kid, and he was used to being cold. His father kept the tenement like an ice-box, always claiming that that they didn't have the money to pay large bills. Not that it stopped him gambling every day at the dog fights.

"I'm never going back there…" Luis muttered. "I'd rather die. I'd rather die!"

"You shouldn't talk to yourself," said a voice from the far side of the fire. "Folks'll think you're crazy. They'll lock you up and throw away the key!"

Luis peered through the flames, but they were too intense for him to see the man who was addressing him, so he wandered around the fire. The man was sitting on the ground, leaning back against a substantial pile of timbers; more fuel for the fire. But this man was certainly not the one who'd collected the wood, for he had no arms. There were not even stumps.

"What are you staring at?"

"Your…arms!"

"I don't have none, boy!" the man replied.

"No, so I see."

"Can't see something I ain't got!" And then seeing the nervous look on Luis' face, he started laughing. "I'm joking with you, you little shrimp. Come here. Sit down.

I ain't gonna strangle you. Might stomp you to death."
Again an outburst of laughter. "Nah, I won't do that neither. Sit! Sit! I'm Nefer the Coffin-Maker. Who the hell
are you?"

"I'm Luis."

"Pleased to make your acquaintance, Luis. Where do
you live?"

"Why'd you want to know?"

"Cause I plan to go there and murder your family,
what do you think? No, kid. I'm just making conversation
is all!"

"I live in the tenements."

"You're a long way from home."

"Can't be far enough for me!"

"I know how you feel. Who needs those people? I got
company here. Not much, but it's enough."

"I don't see anybody!"

"Griegat," Nefer said. "Show yourself."

Luis sensed a movement in the shadows behind the
armless man, and a figure loomed into view, his head
bestial, his hands huge and surely capable of murder.

"Wh…who's this?"

"My only friend. My creature. Griegat."

"What do you mean: your creature?"

"He…made…me," the beast-man said.

"Made you? How?"

Griegat shook his huge head.

Nefer couldn't see his companion but he knew what it
was doing. "He can't tell you how he was made, because
he wasn't there. But I'll tell you."

"Griegat feed the fire."

The creature dragged his heavy frame over to the pile of timbers. He picked up several blocks of wood, loaded them onto his shoulders, and carried them over to the fire, where he dumped them in the flames. It was a prodigious show of strength.

"Where did you find him?" Luis wanted to know.

"I didn't find him," the armless man replied. "I told you. I made him."

"I don't understand."

"He's a golem, lad."

Luis looked at the man blankly.

"You don't know what a golem is?"

"No. I don't."

"It's a creature raised out of the dirt, by magic. I shaped the thing from the very ash beneath our feet, then I mixed it with some of my blood, some of my spit, and I wrote the name of Jehovah upon it, to put the spirit of life into it. Now it serves my every need, don't you, Griegat?"

"Yes, sir."

"Nor do I have to feed it or give it time to sleep."

"It doesn't sleep?"

"No, it lives to serve me, night and day. And it will do so until its life-force fails it."

"What then?"

"I'll make another."

Luis laughed. "This is just a stupid joke!" he said. "You have no arms! How could you make such a thing?"

"You'd be surprised," he said, raising his feet in front of his face, and paring the toes of one with a knife held in the other. It was an impressive display.

"Believe me, he's my handiwork." the man said. "Every inch of him. It took a lot of sweat and patience, but it was worth it. My life without him would be immeasurably harder."

"Could you teach me?" Luis said. "How to make a golem, for myself."

Nefer stared at him, with a small smile playing on his lips. "Why else are you here?" the armless man replied. "Fate brought you here so that you could learn from me."

THE LESSON IN golem-making took almost three weeks. Every day Luis made his way from the tenements to the old furnaces, and every day the armless man gave over his secrets. Words and signs and ceremonies. Needless to say, Luis' constant departures from home and the filthy state in which he returned did not go unnoticed. His father asked questions, and when they were answered with shrugs Luis got several beatings. But the bruises didn't dissuade him. He went to see Nefer, and learned his lessons like a good student, until at last the armless man said: "Tomorrow will be your last day, Luis."

"You mean I'll be ready?"

"You'll be ready."

The next day when he got to Nefer's little encampment he found the armless man had gone, and so had the golem Griegat. The blackened pot in which Griegat had cooked rat stew had gone, along with the filthy bedding on which Nefer slept. All that was left was the ashes of the great bonfire that had first drawn Luis to this place.

And scribbled in those ashes (presumably by Nefer's foot) was one word.

BEGIN

That was what Luis did. He began by performing the ceremony of sanctification that Nefer had taught him. Then he found himself an old can that Nefer had left amongst his garbage and he went to the furnaces to get rain-water to mix with the ash. He added a bladderful of his own water so that the golem would have something of him in it, and his spit too, and his sweat as he worked.

It was hard labor, making enough mud to shape a full-sized man, there in the ground. But Luis was the equal of the task. He worked through the high heat of the day and into the cool of the evening. Then he lit a fire close by the place where the golem lay and he continued to work by the light of the flickering flames. The heat of the fire began to dry the creature as he worked. Bitter steam rose from its form, stinging Luis' eyes. He let his tears run down his cheeks and add their little sum of fluid to the sweat and spit that were already part of the golem's stuff.

Finally he began to recite the words of life that Nefer the armless had taught him, and as he did so he inscribed the name of the creator on the brow of the creature. As he did so he had his first indication that the work he'd done would bear fruit, as the letters of the creator's name sank into the flesh of the creature, and became invisible to the naked eye.

Then, when the words were said, and the letters were written, he sat down in the dirt and allowed fatigue to overtake him. His eyes closed, and for what seemed like just a few moments he drifted off into sleep. When he woke, he knew an hour or more must have passed, however. The fire had burned much lower, and the night sky was a starless black above.

He turned to admire his golem. But it had gone! He scrambled to his feet, his heart beating fearfully. Where was it?

He looked round, half afraid the creature would pounce on him out of the darkness. But then his gaze caught sight of it, standing maybe twenty yards away, staring out towards the tenements. Had it read his mind while he slept? Did it know what he wanted it to do?

"That's where we're going," he said to it. "That's where my family lives. *I want you to kill my family.*"

"Kill them?" the golem said, its voice like stone.

"Yes. And I want to see them all dead. You understand me?"

"Yes. You want to see your family dead."

"Will you do this?"

"You are my Maker. I will do anything my Master asks of me!"

They set out, there and then. Left the last of the fire to burn itself out and headed back through the filthy dirt towards the outskirts of the city.

When they got to the apartment it was that darkened hour of the night when the moon had dropped from sight and the sun had not yet risen, so the darkness is utter.

The golem broke open the apartment door and without waiting for any further instructions from its master it began to go from room to room and shed blood. It was terrifyingly effective. In a matter of moments the job was almost complete. Luis' parents were murdered as they

41

rose from their beds, their heads twisted from their necks and casually tossed aside. His brother and sisters were the next to go, their slaughter thankfully quick but still bloody, horribly bloody.

At last, it was done. Luis felt nothing. Not satisfaction. Not repulsion.

"Let's get out of here," he said.

"First you," the golem said.

Luis thought for a moment that the golem was being polite, ushering him out of the house ahead. But then those huge hands—hands he himself had shaped, taking care with each and every finger—reached out for him and caught his head in their vise.

"What are you doing?" he said.

"You're of the family too," the golem said, and before his Maker could contradict this observation Luis' skull cracked like an egg, spilling blood and thought and fragments of bone down over the golem's hands and arms.

It was purely by chance that Tom Requiem found the creature wandering in the streets of that city, some nights later, and saw in its brutal form and blood-stained skin the making of a profitable monster. He called him, for no better reason than that he liked the name, Elijah. And though he was kind to the creature (kinder than to most others, for some reason) the golem was never tamed from that day forth. It had killed its Maker by its Maker's instructions (as some have said Man has done to God) and was now a brute forever, hungry and vicious. Only sometimes, when the Parade was moving on, and the camp's fires of the night before were being extinguished—ashes trickled over the remains of flames—only then did the golem occasionally show some tiny clue to some pro-found feeling.

It would watch the ashes wither and the wind carry them away, and let out a low tender moan, as though it wished it could be unmade with similar ease and carried off into nothingness.

Dr. Fetter's Family of Freaks

THE PRIVATE DETECTIVE'S name was Ralph Dietrick, and the credo by which he lived was simple: no case was ever dropped until it was solved. In his thirty years of detecting he'd had his share of strange cases but none stranger than the one that came his way one wet afternoon in late November. A man appeared at his office, rain running down his smooth sallow skin.

Dietrick liked to characterize clients in terms of animals (*There ain't a man born*, he'd boast, *who don't resemble an animal if you look at 'em right*). This one was a lizard, no question. A cold-blooded little squirt of a man, who licked his lips all the time (sure sign of a liar, Dietrick thought) and whose eyes were half-popped from his skull, and moved uncannily round and about, like they weren't properly fixed in his head.

"I'm Hubert Fetter," he said. "Doctor Hubert Fetter."

"Oh yeah," said Dietrick. "And what can I do for you?"

"Well, see, here's the thing! I had this collection, see, and it was stolen. And I heard around town that you were the best detective in North Dakota, and I should engage you to search for…what I lost…because you'll find it double quick."

"Well, I ain't making no guarantees regarding the speed of my investigation, Doctor."

"I see."

"But I can tell you this. I never did give up on an investigation. Not once. It took me thirteen years one time to track down a woman I'd been paid to find. I never give up."

"Well, that's good to hear, Dietrick. See, my problem is a little out of the ordinary."

"Oh yeah? What is it you lost?"

"I lost my freaks."

"Your freaks?"

"Yes, I have a family of freaks, and they've been stolen from me. I want them back, Dietrick. They're my pride and joy, those things. I love 'em with all my heart." He took out an unsavory looking handkerchief and wiped his face with it. "My life's not worth living without 'em."

"Well then, you'd better give me a description of 'em."

Fetter supplied the details and the detective got about his work. The trail was not completely cold. After four days Dietrick located a man who sold a car to one of Fetter's freaks.

"Made me sick just to look at the thing!" the man told Dietrick. "It had two heads, this thing. And it looked like it would have jumped me and sucked the blood out of me if I'd turned my back on it."

Once he had a description of the vehicle the freaks were driving, Dietrick simply used his contacts in the police department to have it traced. Two days later, in the early evening, he arrived at a small motel far to the north of the city, where he observed Fetter's freaks coming and going from room 7. Of their abductor there was no sign.

Dietrick didn't make his presence known. He simply called Doctor Fetter, who arrived some hours later in a scruffy motor truck. Only then did he show himself.

"Didn't I tell you I'd find 'em for you?" he said, standing at the door of the single room where all the freaks had been living together. It stank of rotted food, of excrement, but most of all of the bodies of the freaks themselves, which seemed to give off a particularly pungent sweat.

"You did indeed," said Doctor Fetter. "Good job! Good job!" He reached into his jacket and took out a strangely decorated wallet.

"You're the one turned us in?" said one of the two heads that sprouted from the neck of the larger of the freaks.

"Why'd you do that?" said the other head.

"I didn't turn you in," Dietrick said. "I saved you."

"From what?" said a thing no bigger than a foetus that lay on pillows at the head of the bed. "We ran away from that sonofabitch, Fetter!"

"He used us!" said a diminutive woman who stood close to Dietrick. Her tears made her mascara run. "He experiments on us and then when we die, he puts us in jars and exhibits us. Or else skins us!"

"She's crazy!" Fetter protested. "I am a civilized man. I'd never do such a thing!"

The woman suddenly ran towards Fetter and snatched the wallet from his hand, opening it up to display its design.

"He skinned my husband when he died after one of his experiments. Look! Look! This tattoo was on his chest!"

There on the wallet (which did indeed have the texture of tanned human skin) was a heart tattoo with an arrow passing through it. "Aaron loves Tiny Alice" was written on the heart.

"Alice, shut up!" Fetter said, and then realizing that in his fury he'd let the truth out, he snatched his wallet from Tiny Alice and pulled a handful of bills from it. "Here, here, take it all!" he said, pressing the money on Dietrick. "Just forget what you saw here and go."

"Don't," the freak on the pillow begged. "Don't you see how angry he is now? The moment you leave, Fetter will kill us and breed more!"

"Ridiculous." Fetter said. "They're cretins, Mister Dietrick, that's the tragic truth. Brains the size of peas. But who's to argue with Nature, eh? All I do—out of the kindness of my heart—is give them a place to lay their weary bones."

Dietrick looked at them one more time—at their loose, drooling mouths, at their monstrously misshapen bodies—and he shook his head.

"Cretins, huh?" he said.

"Human refuse."

And yet their eyes, Dietrick thought, their eyes. They were filled with feeling, and with a sad but marvelous intelligence.

"You know what?" he said to Fetter. "Maybe I should stick around awhile."

"What for?"

"Just to make sure these folks are getting treated kindly."

"I don't like your implication, Dietrick. Take your money and get out of here. Go on!"

"No"—said the two-headed creature who was closest to the door—"please stay!"

"Shut up!" Fetter said, and delivered the creature a back-handed blow that threw it across the room. Then he glanced back at the detective. "Are you still here?" he said. "I told you: go! This isn't your business."

"You lied to me," Dietrick said.

"What if I did?"

"They weren't abducted at all."

"Don't start getting sentimental, Dietrick. You've got your money—"

"I'm not interested in your money." Dietrick pressed past Fetter and went to where the struck freak now lay, sprawled on the floor. "Here," he said, offering the creature his hand.

The thing shook its heads. "You'd best go, mister," one of them said. The other agreed. "Go quick. The Doctor, he no play fair."

"I'm not scared of Fetter," Dietrick said.

"You should be, mister," said the first head. "You'll get into trouble if you help us."

"Go! Please go!"

As it spoke, its four eyes slid away from Dietrick's face and focused on something behind him.

Dietrick turned, instinctively raising his hand in front of his face to ward off a blow from Fetter. But it was not a blow that was coming his way; it was a hypodermic needle. It plunged into the meat of his hand and emerged on the other side, piercing his eye. With the hypodermic pinned to his face, Dietrick fell back against the wall. Fetter was on him in an instant, pressing the hypodermic's plunger. Its contents surged into Dietrick's bloodstream.

"Oh God…" Dietrick said, "…what have you…?"

He didn't finish the question. The drug Fetter had put into him had already turned his tongue to lead.

"I told you to leave," Fetter said as the detective slid down the wall. "But no. You had to be the hero, didn't you?" He shook his head. "Stupid. Stupid. Stupid!"

HOW MANY HOURS went by before the experiment began? Or was it days perhaps? Dietrick no longer knew. He couldn't speak, he couldn't defend himself, he couldn't even piss or shit. The doctor had control of him, utterly, utterly, and everything that passed in front of him did so like a kind of dream. No, not a dream. A nightmare…

Fetter came at him with a hundred hypodermics, and filled his flesh with some transforming fluid. Fetter watched him as his drugs took their terrible effect. Dietrick shrank in his skin, decades of decrepitude claiming his flesh, his bone, his marrow.

Only when it was all over, and his body had become a contorted broken thing, did Doctor Fetter proffer a mirror, so that Dietrick could see with his one good eye the abomination he had become. He let out a wordless howl that woke others all through the Doctor's Chamber of Transformation: a ragged chorus of melancholia that went on and on and on till there was no strength left in their twisted forms.

Infernal Parade

In the end, mercifully, Fetter lowered his suffering monster into a jar of formaldehyde. It burned as it filled Dietrick's lungs, but through the pain he heard Fetter boasting, of what glories the future held, of how they were all to be part of some Infernal Parade. Fetter's insane boasts meant nothing to Dietrick. The last thought that passed through his head as death overcame him was that there had never been anyone in his life, man or woman, who had cared about him enough to send someone looking for him, the way he had been sent, over the years. Undetected, then, he died.

And in time Doctor Fetter's Family of Freaks— swelled by one—joined the Infernal Parade.

The
Sabbaticus

IN THE WASTELANDS of Thyle there is a city called Karantica. Once mighty, it is now deserted. Lizards bask on the sun-baked plazas, undisturbed by the tread of human feet. Wild dogs fight and bleed and die in the great houses of that city, where every day was once filled with beauty and music and the high talk of great philosophers.

What happened to Karantica? What was the calamity that overcame the city? Some horrendous plague, was it? Some civil war, that set great families one against the other, and in the process emptied the city of its inhabitants?

There are historians who believe both explanations are true, but there is another explanation which is worthy of our attention. It has never been set down until now, existing only in the form of rumors and gossip.

First, let me explain that Karantica was in the time of its greatness a city ruled over by priests, not potentates. Religion subdued its people, rather than the rule of civil law. The laws of the Gods of Karantica were cruel, no question: the judgments passed down through their intercedents in the priest class were often unspeakably vicious. Blinding and castrations were demanded for very minor offences, and female felons who'd been condemned to death were often taken into the temple on the night before their executions, where—according to the accounts of the celibate priests—the Gods sent monstrous creatures to violate them, and tear at their flesh. Even children were not exempt from the judgments of Karantica's deities. They were regularly cooked alive in the bellies of iron dragons for inconsequential crimes.

Not everyone was happy with the cruelty of the Gods. Far from it.

When one Judge Phio opened his people's court in the filthy streets of Karantica's poorest district, the Myassa, he found people more than willing to hear his New Theory of the Law. Justice should not be cruel, he said. A civilized society—and what city in the Underland laid greater claim to being cultured than Karantica?—did not cook the flesh of a living child for the "crime" of stealing a fish from the fountains outside the Great Temple. The law, to be respected, needed to balance forcefulness with compassion. There was a better way to be just, Phio said. A human way.

The people of Karantica weren't stupid. They saw the sense in what he said. And word of his uncommon love of common sense quickly spread. Rather than take their disputes to the priests, people instead began to present themselves to Phio for judgment, their numbers swelling so quickly that in a matter of weeks his little court was hopelessly over-booked and he would often work from six in the morning to midnight, dispensing his particular brand of what he called "honest law."

His presence did not go unnoticed, of course. The priests had spies everywhere around the city, and word soon reached them of this man and his heretical vision of justice. The priests, led by the most vicious of the great punishers, Thamut-ul-mire, met in secret conclave to determine what should be done to bring this problem to an end. It was only a matter of time, they agreed, before this Judge Phio's heresies spread, and these courts began to proliferate. The answer's simple, said some of the older priests: accuse Phio of taking the law of the Gods into mortal hands—which he is undeniably doing—and then having Thamut-ul-mire conceive of some public death for him so lingering and so horrible that nobody will ever try his tricks again.

"It won't work," Thamut-ul-mire said quietly. "We'll make a martyr of him."

"Well, what do you suggest?" one of the Elders asked.

"That we punish the people for listening to him," Thamut-ul-mire replied.

"Punish the people? All the people?"

"Yes."

The Elder laughed. "How do you suggest we do that? "Have half of them flog the other half and then flog the floggers?"

"No, nothing so crude," Thamut-ul-mire replied. "Fear is what we'll use to bring them back to us."

"Fear of the Gods?"

Thamut-ul-mire shook his head. "Fear of that which is not the Gods," he replied.

THREE NIGHTS LATER, just after nightfall, three children, two brothers and their little sister, playing in an orchard close to the edge of the city, were murdered under the pithik trees. Not just murdered but, disassembled and disembow-eled, their brains scooped out of the cups of their skulls and eaten, their tender innards unwound and left trailing in the grass. What kind of man would do such a thing? People wanted to know. It was beyond comprehension.

Two nights later, seven more children were slaugh-tered. This time all of different families, in the streets of a well-heeled district occupied by merchants and their families. The deaths resembled in every way the deaths of the three children murdered in the orchard. The same brutal unknitting of the bodies, the same removing of the brains and the innards left trailing. This time, however, the miscreant was glimpsed as it shambled away from the scene of its depravities. It was not human; not remotely. A great reptilian beast that had apparently come into the city from the wilderness. It was a creature that the citi-zens of Karantica knew by name: a Sabbaticus. Word of its presence spread through the city. This was not just any scavenger. This was a beast out of the Testaments of Jidadia, the great religious book which the priests went to when they were seeking guidance as to how a certain miscreant needed to be judged. It fed on the thoughts of children, and on the despair of their parents.

"This is what you have unleashed," Thamut-ul-mire shouted from his pulpit the next day. "By following laws other than those brought to you by your priests—the laws of the Gods!—you have invited into our once safe streets this abomination of the Wilderness."

The thousand-strong congregation fell to its knees, some of the worshippers uttering cries of "Save us! Save us!" Others simply let out sobs, that echoed around the dome of the Great Temple.

"I cannot save you against your own sin!" Thamut-ul-mire returned. "Only you can do that!"

"Tell us how!"

"There is a certain man in this city who has set his laws above those of the Gods. Perhaps if you turned your backs on him, this creature, this Sabbaticus would leave Karantica alone and return to the Wilderness from whence your corruptions called it!"

The crowd rose as one, their sobs and their entreaties turning to howls for vengeance. They went through the city gathering weapons along the way, the crowd's numbers swelling as word of what had transpired at the Temple spread. In his makeshift courthouse in the Myassa, Judge Phio heard the roar of the mob as it approached. His supporters had already brought him warning, of course. He knew what would happen to him when the crowd kicked down the door and dragged him out. If he'd been quick and lucky perhaps he might have escaped, but where would he have gone? Karantica was the city where he'd been born and raised. He loved it with all his heart, and he loved its poor manipulated people. Which was not to say that he was happy to die now. Not with so much work to do. But he was ready to face the consequences of what he'd done.

Judge Phio's death was not quick. The people of Karantica were expert from past stonings at the craft of keeping a man from perishing too quickly. For two hours and seven minutes Phio suffered in the sun, his left eye dashed from its socket, all broken, his robes soaked red from neck to hem. The blow-flies and the blood-bees swarmed around him in their many thousands, and settled on his ruined face until he was entirely black with them. At last, he dropped to his knees, and minutes later fell forward. There was a curious silence then, and stillness, until a small boy, no more than five or six, ran forward and gleefully proceeded to stamp on Phio's head. The rest of the crowd—many of whom were alive today thanks to the compassion of the man they had beneath their feet—escalated the fury of the tarantella.

When it was done—when the judge had breathed his last, every bone in his body shattered—they were not ashamed that they had killed their savior.

After all, had he not brought the Sabbaticus out of the Wilderness? He deserved his death.

The priests' spies returned to the Great Temple quickly, with news of what had happened. They were paid off, and sent on their way.

"Good," said the Elder, "it's done. We have no more need of subterfuge."

"What should we do about the men that killed the children?"

"Bury them alive, out in the Wilderness," Thamut-ul-mire said. "I'll see it done. And I'll have priests with me to help me do the job. We'll have no more dealings with paid assassins."

It was so agreed. That night the two professionals who had been hired to kill the children—and with the aid of a little theatrics, throw the shadow of the beast on a wall here and there, and leave its tracks in the blood of the dead children—were abducted from their huts down by the river and taken out under cover of darkness into the windy wastes that lay all about Karantica. They were given shovels, and told to dig a single hole, large enough for two corpses. They knew they were digging their own graves, but they were too afraid of how Thamut-ul-mire might affect their lives after death to contradict his instructions. As helpless as the children whose lives they had taken, they did as they were instructed, digging their graves and then jumping down into the hole together. The priests then threw down on top of them the crude machinery of their deceptions: the puppets that had cast the flittering shadows of the Sabbaticus on the wall and the blocks of carved wood they'd used to create a trail in blood.

Finally, at Thamut-ul-mire's instruction, his fellow priests proceeded to bury the men. Only then, when the dirt began to patter down on their faces, did the murderers begin to voice their fear, sobbing and begging for mercy. None was forthcoming, of course; and after a time the sheer weight of dirt smothered them, and they were silenced.

"Let's return to the Temple," Thamut-ul-mire said. "This wind makes my teeth ache."

He had no sooner finished speaking than the wind gusted particularly hard, and the flames in the priests' lamps went out, and the moon slipped behind a dust cloud that was looming in the east. In the sudden murk, the priest heard the sound of something moving nearby, and a foul stench stung their nostrils.

"What is that?" one of them said, his voice betraying a veneer of unease.

"Some animal heard the screams," Thamut-ul-mire replied. "Come back to scavenge no doubt."

"What animal?" the priest replied.

"Who cares what animal?" the other said. "Let's be gone."

THE TERRIBLE CYCLE of deaths began that very night. Thirteen children died. Another nineteen died the night after. Thirty-six the night after that. The grotesque sights that subsequent dawns presented left the people of the city in no doubt as to the identity of the murderer. The Sabbaticus wasn't satisfied with the death of Judge Phio.

The congregation came beating at the doors of the Great Temple, demanding answers from their priests. Why, if they had punished Phio for his crimes, had the Sabbaticus escalated its war against the innocents of Karantica? It wanted blood on blood on blood on blood.

Sealed up in the darkness of the Temple, the priests debated how they could possibly answer the question without touching upon the truth of the matter, which to them was all too clear: the wind had carried word of their deceits out into the Wilderness, and the Sabbaticus had come from the wastes to see what crimes were being done in its name, and to prove that it could do worse.

Why, it could even kill priests.

That very night, in fact, it came up through the tunnels that ran beneath the Temple and it broke the legendary rules of its nature. It killed grown men, instead of children.

And instead of eating their brains it ate that part that made them men.

When the doors of the Great Temple were finally opened, and the massacre within discovered—eleven hundred and two priests slaughtered—a great exodus from the city began.

Nobody stayed. Not a single soul.

What was the use? However beautiful Karantica was—however fine its palaces and mansions, however exquisite its plazas and boulevards—it was a cursed city. Neither children nor priests were safe there.

Better the Wilderness than Karantica, people took to saying. And the saying spread, and was never forgotten, even after the Sabbaticus had left the city and been tamed by Tom Requiem, becoming in time part of the Infernal Parade's great entertainment.

Bethany
Bled

BETHANY BLED HAD been washing clothes down at the river when the man on the dappled horse had ridden up to her and told her that she was the most beautiful woman in all of Delphi. She was not used to flattery. The daughter of a charcoal burner, and illegitimate at that, she had never known the company of a man who could weave words so exquisitely as the Duke Delphi. For the next several days he made secret assignations with her, and by the time Sunday came, she was ready to give her heart and soul and body to him. They met under the yews in the churchyard, where the many dead of the village were laid in humble graves.

"Lie with me here," he said to her.

She was astonished at how forward he was, and even more astonished at how easily she fell for his fine words and gentle manners. She lay with him, there in the lush grass beneath the spreading yew trees, and within a matter of minutes he had talked her out of her clothes, and was upon her, having his way.

There was precious little pleasure in it for her, at least in the doing of the deed. But afterwards, when he parted from her, she thought of him over and over, and imagined his eyes upon her neck and breasts, and heard the promises he had made to her.

"I will marry you," he'd said to her as he'd unbuttoned her bodice, "and you'll be the most beautiful Duchess Delphi that ever lived and you'll want for nothing."

"For nothing."

"For nothing."

NINETEEN TIMES HE had made love to her, on several occasions in the churchyard, and once in the church itself, there on the hard, cold floor. But she had not cared that the floor was cold, or that he sometimes bruised her in his ardor: his promises made everything right. He loved her, he swore, loved her as no man had ever loved a woman, back to the beginning of the world.

"Shall we be man and wife?" she'd asked him.

"Of course," he had said.

"When?"

"In time."

That was what he always said when she asked him— in time, in time, but as the weeks went by his promises began to falter. He still made his demands of her (and she, still flattered that she had gained the attention of so mighty a man, still gave in to him). She wasn't stupid, however. She knew that it was only a matter of time before her fine Duke deserted her completely. She had to do something about it, had to find some way to hold onto him. But how?

There was a woman who lived on the outskirts of the village known as Old Etta. Nobody spoke to her much when she went about in the streets. But she had heard that when some of the young women wanted babies, or a man needed to curse the cattle of a neighbor, it was to Old Etta that they went for their means. Bethany went to her one midnight, and explained her situation.

The old woman listened and then said: "What do you need from me?"

"Some herb that will make me love him always, so that he'll never desert me."

"I doubt such an herb exists," Old Etta replied. "But I might have something that would help you, I suppose."

"Please, please, please give it to me. I don't care about the cost."

"Ah, listen to her! So indifferent to the price of things!" The woman gave Bethany a toothless grin. "Didn't your Mama teach you that everything comes with a price, girl?"

Old Etta didn't wait for a reply, but went to the table, where a number of small pots and jars were assembled. She took a pinch of the contents of three pots, and deposited them in a small purse of undyed linen.

"Sleep one night with this between your legs," she said as she passed it over, "and you will have some consequence of it. This I guarantee."

"Thank you," Bethany said, and, paying the woman, hurried away.

She did as the old woman had instructed and slept with the little purse of bitter-smelling herbs between her legs. The Duke did not visit her the next day, or the day after, nor the day after that, and when he did finally appear Bethany was sure any effect the old woman's magic might have had would surely have faded, but no sooner had he lain with her than Bethany had proof that her purchase had been worth its price.

"Bethany," the Duke said, "I love you."

"Yes?"

"Bethany. I love you."

"Well, that's good. So—"

"Bethany. I love you."

"Please, Lord. Say something other than—"

"Bethany. I love you."

But he could not. The words were all he had in his skull apparently. He uttered them over and over and over until his voice grew hoarse. And while he uttered them he made love to her, over and over and over. She soon began to tire of his attentions and of the ceaseless professions of love that accompanied them, and struggled to be free of him.

"Bethany, I love you," he said as she pulled herself out from underneath him.

"Bethany, I love you," he said as he followed her out of the churchyard apparently unconcerned that he wore nothing but his arousal.

"Bethany, I love you," he said as he followed her down into the village to the door of her house, which she finally slammed in his perfect face.

That was where his followers found him an hour later, his throat so ragged from repeating his words of love that he spoke blood instead of syllables. They didn't ask for an explanation. They simply covered their master's nakedness, and took him home.

Witch-hunters came for Bethany Bled the next day, with their menaces and their pricking-forks and their comprehensive price-lists for what a guilty witch might be expected to pay for the service of being flogged and branded and burned.

Bethany was summarily accused of diabolical works. She denied them fiercely, of course. They put her to the rack. And soon she was admitting everything.

Poor Old Etta was burned quickly and without trial. Too many men and women, high and mighty, had profited from her love-phials and her poisons to want her to have any chance to speak about what she'd done. But Bethany's death was not to be so quiet or kind.

For six nights they kept her in the darkness of her dungeon, until at last she heard a key in the lock, and the great oak door swung open, and a man—withered and twitching—was carried into the filthy cell. Only when he spoke did the prisoner recognize her visitor.

"Bethany, I love you," he croaked.

It was the Duke! My god, she thought, look at him! So reduced! So dried up and frail, his beauty gone, his youth gone, all wasted away in the space of a week or two. So much for love. His continued expressions of devotion towards her could not save her, of course.

They brought her out, into the great torture chamber, where stood tormenting implements of every kind. The rack they'd stretched her on, braziers with brands, heated white in the embers. Weights and ropes for the strappado; a common garrote; axes, of course, for the restraint of hands and feet and the lopping of heads.

And an Iron Maiden, sometimes called the Maiden of Nuremberg. A device made in the likeness of a woman, into which the prisoner was put, and all closed up, so that in its confines they would die a long slow death, pierced through by the spikes that were arranged upon the interior of the monstrous device.

The Duke pointed towards it.

"Bethany, I love you," he said. Though his tongue had no choice but to speak words of affection, his gesture was clear enough. It was a death sentence. He intended to see her die inside the Iron Maiden.

The priests began to recite a prayer, as she was dragged to the Maiden. But their pieties could not drown out the Duke's crazed repetitions.

"Bethany, I love you."

"Bethany, I love you."

"Bethany, I love you."

They closed the door on her. The pain as the spikes pierced her body made her scream, a shrill scream that echoed back and forth inside her hot prison.

Sitting close to the Maiden, rocking back and forth, the Duke kept up his litany of love, as Bethany's blood poured from the bottom of the monstrous device. Only when the crawling red blood had reached his feet did he finally fall silent, and allow himself to be carried away.

In the agonizing darkness, pungent with the smell of her blood and entrails, Bethany heard a voice say:

"Want to join us?"

Who was speaking to her? Some devil, was it, come up out of Hell to claim her sinning soul? No, it wasn't a devil. She wasn't dead. She could still feel the spikes piercing her through and through.

"Who are you?" she murmured.

"My name is Tom Requiem," the man said, "and we've come to bring you to join our Infernal Parade, if you care to do so?"

"Am I not dead?"

Infernal Parade

"Alive? Dead? Who cares? We don't concern ourselves with such petty distinctions. But better hurry if you want to come. We have to get you and your show-piece out of here before first light."

"My show-piece?" said Bethany.

"Your Maiden," said Requiem. "Your beautiful Maiden."

How could she refuse? It was better than hell, wasn't it, to be out on the road playing out her Death and Resurrection nightly for the entertainment of those who had the good fortune to meet the Infernal Parade upon the road? And who knew? Perhaps she'd find somebody else to love her somewhere along the way. Someone that she wouldn't have to connive with charms to make them tell her they loved her; and would forgive her the wounds in her flesh, and the coldness of her skin, if she loved them truly in return.